The Bar Sinister

Miss Dorothy snatches me up and kisses me between the ears.

THE BAR SINISTER

BY

RICHARD HARDING DAVIS

ILLUSTRATED BY

E. M. ASHE

NEW YORK

CHARLES SCRIBNER'S SONS

1903

PREFACE

WHEN this story first appeared, the writer received letters of two kinds, one asking a question and the other making a statement. The question was, whether there was any foundation of truth in the story; the statement challenged him to say that there was. The letters seemed to show that a large proportion of readers prefer their dose of fiction with a sweetening of fact. This is written to furnish that condiment, and to answer the question and the statement.

In the dog world, the original of the bull-terrier in the story is known as Edgewood Cold Steel and to his intimates as " Kid." His father was Lord Minto, a thoroughbred bull-terrier, well known in Canada, but the story of Kid's life is that his mother was a black-and-tan named Vic. She was a lady of doubtful pedigree. Among her offspring by Lord Minto, so I have been often informed by many Canadian dog-fanciers, breeders, and exhibitors, was the only white puppy, Kid, in a litter of black-and-tans. He made his first appearance in the show world in 1900 in Toronto, where, under the judging of Mr. Charles H. Mason, he was easily first. During that year, when he came to our kennels, and in the two years following, he carried off many blue ribbons and cups at nearly every first-class show in the country. The other dog, " Jimmy Jocks," who in the book was his friend and mentor, was in real life his friend and companion, Woodcote Jumbo, or "Jaggers," an aristocratic son of a long line of English champions. He has gone to that place where some day all good dogs must go.

In this autobiography I have tried

to describe Kid as he really is, and
this year, when he again strives for
blue ribbons, I trust, should the gentle
reader see him at any of the bench-
shows, he will give him a friendly
pat and make his acquaintance.
He will find his advances met with a
polite and gentle courtesy.

THE AUTHOR

Illustrations

✤

The Bar Sinister

THE BAR SINISTER

PART I

HE Master was walking most unsteady, his legs tripping each other. After the fifth or sixth round, my legs often go the same way.

But even when the Master's legs bend and twist a bit, you mustn't think he can't reach you. Indeed, that is the time he kicks most frequent. So I kept behind him in the shadow, or ran in the middle of the street. He stopped at many public

houses with swinging doors, those
doors that are cut so high from the
sidewalk that you can look in under
them, and see if the Master is inside.
At night, when I peep beneath them,
the man at the counter will see me
first and say, " Here's the Kid, Jerry,
come to take you home. Get a move
on you"; and the Master will stumble
out and follow me. It's lucky for us
I'm so white, for, no matter how
dark the night, he can always see me
ahead, just out of reach of his boot.
At night the Master certainly does
see most amazing. Sometimes he
sees two or four of me, and walks in
a circle, so that I have to take him by
the leg of his trousers and lead him

4

The Master will stumble out and follow me.

into the right road. One night, when he was very nasty-tempered and I was coaxing him along, two men passed us, and one of them says, "Look at that brute!" and the other asks, "Which?" and they both laugh. The Master he cursed them good and proper.

But this night, whenever we stopped at a public house, the Master's pals left it and went on with us to the next. They spoke quite civil to me, and when the Master tried a flying kick, they gives him a shove. "Do you want us to lose our money?" says the pals.

I had had nothing to eat for a day and a night, and just before we set

out the Master gives me a wash under the hydrant. Whenever I am
locked up until all the slop-pans in
our alley are empty, and made to
take a bath, and the Master's pals
speak civil and feel my ribs, I know
something is going to happen. And
that night, when every time they see
a policeman under a lamp-post, they
dodged across the street, and when
at the last one of them picked me up
and hid me under his jacket, I began
to tremble; for I knew what it meant.
It meant that I was to fight again for
the Master.

I don't fight because I like fighting.
I fight because if I didn't the other dog
would find my throat, and the Master

6

would lose his stakes, and I would be very sorry for him, and ashamed. Dogs can pass me and I can pass dogs, and I'd never pick a fight with none of them. When I see two dogs standing on their hind legs in the streets, clawing each other's ears, and snapping for each other's windpipes, or howling and swearing and rolling in the mud, I feel sorry they should act so, and pretend not to notice. If he'd let me, I'd like to pass the time of day with every dog I meet. But there's something about me that no nice dog can abide. When I trot up to nice dogs, nodding and grinning, to make friends, they always tell me to be off. "Go to the devil!" they bark at me. "Get out!" And when I walk away they shout "Mongrel!" and "Gutter-dog!" and sometimes, after my back is turned, they rush me. I could kill most of them with three shakes, breaking the back-bone of the little ones and squeezing the throat of the big ones. But what's the good? They *are* nice dogs; that's why I try to make up to them: and, though it's not for them to say it, I *am* a street-dog, and if I try to push into the company of my betters, I suppose it's their right to teach me my place.

Of course they don't know I'm the best fighting bull-terrier of my weight in Montreal. That's why it

8

wouldn't be fair for me to take notice of what they shout. They don't know that if I once locked my jaws on them I'd carry away whatever I touched. The night I fought Kelley's White Rat, I wouldn't loosen up until the Master made a noose in my leash and strangled me; and, as for that Ottawa dog, if the handlers hadn't thrown red pepper down my nose I *never* would have let go of him. I don't think the handlers treated me quite right that time, but maybe they didn't know the Ottawa dog was dead. I did.

I learned my fighting from my mother when I was very young. We slept in a lumber-yard on the river-front, and by day hunted for food along the wharves. When we got it, the other tramp-dogs would try to take it off us, and then it was wonderful to see mother fly at them and drive them away. All I know of fighting I learned from mother, watching her picking the ash-heaps for me when I was too little to fight for myself. No one ever was so good to me as mother. When it snowed and the ice was in the St. Lawrence, she used to hunt alone, and bring me back new bones, and she'd sit and laugh to see me trying to swallow 'em whole. I was just a puppy then; my teeth was falling out. When I was able to fight we

kept the whole river-range to our-
selves. I had the genuine long
"punishing" jaw, so mother said,
and there wasn't a man or a dog
that dared worry us. Those were
happy days, those were; and we
lived well, share and share alike, and
when we wanted a bit of fun, we
chased the fat old wharf-rats! My,
how they would squeal!

Then the trouble came. It was no
trouble to me. I was too young to
care then. But mother took it so
to heart that she grew ailing, and
wouldn't go abroad with me by day.
It was the same old scandal that
they're always bringing up against
me. I was so young then that I didn't

know. I couldn't see any difference between mother—and other mothers.

But one day a pack of curs we drove off snarled back some new names at her, and mother dropped her head and ran, just as though they had whipped us. After that she wouldn't go out with me except in the dark, and one day she went away and never came back, and, though I hunted for her in every court and alley and back street of Montreal, I never found her.

One night, a month after mother ran away, I asked Guardian, the old blind mastiff, whose Master is the night watchman on our slip, what it all meant. And he told me.

12

"Every dog in Montreal knows," he says, "except you; and every Master knows. So I think it's time you knew."

Then he tells me that my father, who had treated mother so bad, was a great and noble gentleman from London. "Your father had twenty-two registered ancestors, had your father," old Guardian says, "and in him was the best bull-terrier blood of England, the most ancientest, the most royal; the winning 'blue-ribbon' blood, that breeds champions. He had sleepy pink eyes and thin pink lips, and he was as white all over as his own white teeth, and under his white skin you could see his

13

muscles, hard and smooth, like the links of a steel chain. When your father stood still, and tipped his nose in the air, it was just as though he was saying, 'Oh, yes, you common dogs and men, you may well stare. It must be a rare treat for you colonials to see real English royalty.' He certainly was pleased with hisself, was your father. He looked just as proud and haughty as one of them stone dogs in Victoria Park — them as is cut out of white marble. And you're like him," says the old mastiff — "by that, of course, meaning you're white, same as him. That's the only likeness. But, you see, the trouble is, Kid — well, you see, Kid, the trouble is — your mother —"

14

"That will do," I said, for then I understood without his telling me, and I got up and walked away, holding my head and tail high in the air.

But I was, oh, so miserable, and I wanted to see mother that very minute, and tell her that I didn't care.

Mother is what I am, a street-dog; there's no royal blood in mother's veins, nor is she like that father of mine, nor — and that's the worst — she's not even like me. For while I, when I'm washed for a fight, am as white as clean snow, she — and this is our trouble — she, my mother, is a black-and-tan.

When mother hid herself from me, I was twelve months old and able to take care of myself, and as, after mother left me, the wharves were never the same, I moved uptown and met the Master. Before he came, lots of other men-folks had tried to make up to me, and to whistle me home. But they either tried patting me or coaxing me with a piece of meat; so I didn't take to 'em. But one day the Master pulled me out of a street-fight by the hind legs, and kicked me good.

"You want to fight, do you?" says he. "I'll give you all the *fighting* you want!" he says, and he kicks me again. So I knew he was my Master, and I followed him home. Since that day I've pulled off many fights for him, and they've brought

16

dogs from all over the province to have a go at me; but up to that night none, under thirty pounds, had ever downed me.

But that night, so soon as they carried me into the ring, I saw the dog was overweight, and that I was no match for him. It was asking too much of a puppy. The Master should have known I couldn't do it. Not that I mean to blame the Master, for when sober, which he sometimes was,—though not, as you might say, his habit,—he was most kind to me, and let me out to find food, if I could get it, and only kicked me when I didn't pick him up at night and lead him home.

But kicks will stiffen the muscles, and starving a dog so as to get him ugly-tempered for a fight may make him nasty, but it's weakening to his insides, and it causes the legs to wobble.

The ring was in a hall back of a public house. There was a red-hot whitewashed stove in one corner, and the ring in the other. I lay in the Master's lap, wrapped in my blanket, and, spite of the stove, shivering awful; but I always shiver before a fight: I can't help gettin' excited. While the men-folks were a-flashing their money and taking their last drink at the bar, a little Irish groom in gaiters came up to me and give me the back of his

hand to smell, and scratched me behind the ears.

"You poor little pup," says he;
"you haven't no show," he says.
"That brute in the tap-room he'll
eat your heart out."

"That's what *you* think," says
the Master, snarling. "I'll lay you
a quid the Kid chews him up."

The groom he shook his head, but
kept looking at me so sorry-like that
I begun to get a bit sad myself. He
seemed like he couldn't bear to leave
off a-patting of me, and he says,
speaking low just like he would to a
man-folk, "Well, good luck to you,
little pup," which I thought so civil
of him that I reached up and licked

19

his hand. I don't do that to many men. And the Master he knew I didn't, and took on dreadful.

"What 'ave you got on the back of your hand?" says he, jumping up.

"Soap!" says the groom, quick as a rat. "That's more than you've got on yours. Do you want to smell of it?" and he sticks his fist under the Master's nose. But the pals pushed in between 'em.

"He tried to poison the Kid!" shouts the Master.

"Oh, one fight at a time," says the referee. "Get into the ring, Jerry. We're waiting." So we went into the ring.

I never could just remember what

20

did happen in that ring. He give me
no time to spring. He fell on me like
a horse. I couldn't keep my feet
against him, and though, as I saw,
he could get his hold when he liked,
he wanted to chew me over a bit
first. I was wondering if they'd be
able to pry him off me, when, in the
third round, he took his hold; and I
begun to drown, just as I did when I
fell into the river off the Red C slip.
He closed deeper and deeper on my
throat, and everything went black
and red and bursting; and then,
when I were sure I were dead, the
handlers pulled him off, and the
Master give me a kick that brought
me to. But I couldn't move none, or

even wink, both eyes being shut with lumps.

"He's a cur!" yells the Master, "a sneaking, cowardly cur! He lost the fight for me," says he, "because he's a —— —— —— cowardly cur." And he kicks me again in the lower ribs, so that I go sliding across the sawdust. "There's gratitude fer yer," yells the Master. "I've fed that dog, and nussed that dog and housed him like a prince; and now he puts his tail between his legs and sells me out, he does. He's a coward! I've done with him, I am. I'd sell him for a pipeful of tobacco." He picked me up by the tail, and swung me for the men-folks to see. "Does

22

" He's a coward, I've done with him."

any gentleman here want to buy a dog," he says, "to make into sausage-meat?" he says. "That's all he's good for."

Then I heard the little Irish groom say, "I'll give you ten bob for the dog."

And another voice says, "Ah, don't you do it; the dog's same as dead — mebbe he is dead."

"Ten shillings!" says the Master, and his voice sobers a bit; "make it two pounds and he's yours."

But the pals rushed in again.

"Don't you be a fool, Jerry," they say. "You'll be sorry for this when you're sober. The Kid's worth a fiver."

One of my eyes was not so swelled up as the other, and as I hung by my tail, I opened it, and saw one of the pals take the groom by the shoulder.

"You ought to give 'im five pounds for that dog, mate," he says; "that's no ordinary dog. That dog's got good blood in him, that dog has. Why, his father — that very dog's father —"

I thought he never would go on. He waited like he wanted to be sure the groom was listening.

"That very dog's father," says the pal, "is Regent Royal, son of Champion Regent Monarch, champion bull-terrier of England for four years."

I was sore, and torn, and chewed

24

most awful, but what the pal said sounded so fine that I wanted to wag my tail, only couldn't, owing to my hanging from it.

But the Master calls out: "Yes, his father was Regent Royal; who's saying he wasn't? but the pup's a cowardly cur, that's what his pup is. And why? I'll tell you why: because his mother was a black-and-tan street-dog, that's why!"

I don't see how I got the strength, but, someway, I threw myself out of the Master's grip and fell at his feet, and turned over and fastened all my teeth in his ankle, just across the bone.

When I woke, after the pals had

kicked me off him, I was in the smoking-car of a railroad-train, lying in
the lap of the little groom, and he
was rubbing my open wounds with
a greasy yellow stuff, exquisite to
the smell and most agreeable to lick
off.

PART II

"ELL, what's your name—Nolan? Well, Nolan, these references are satisfactory," said the young gentleman my new Master called "Mr. Wyndham, sir." "I'll take you on as second man. You can begin to-day."

My new Master shuffled his feet and put his finger to his forehead. "Thank you, sir," says he. Then he choked like he had swallowed a fish-bone. "I have a little dawg, sir," says he.

27

"You can't keep him," says "Mr. Wyndham, sir," very short.

"'E's only a puppy, sir," says my new Master; "'e wouldn't go outside the stables, sir."

"It's not that," says "Mr. Wyndham, sir." "I have a large kennel of very fine dogs; they're the best of their breed in America. I don't allow strange dogs on the premises."

The Master shakes his head, and motions me with his cap, and I crept out from behind the door. "I'm sorry, sir," says the Master. "Then I can't take the place. I can't get along without the dawg, sir."

"Mr. Wyndham, sir," looked at me that fierce that I guessed he was going to whip me, so I turned over

28

on my back and begged with my legs
and tail.

"Why, you beat him!" says "Mr.
Wyndham, sir," very stern.

"No fear!" the Master says, getting very red. "The party I bought
him off taught him that. He never
learnt that from me!" He picked me
up in his arms, and to show "Mr.
Wyndham, sir," how well I loved the
Master, I bit his chin and hands.

"Mr. Wyndham, sir," turned over
the letters the Master had given him.
"Well, these references certainly are
very strong," he says. "I guess I'll
let the dog stay. Only see you keep
him away from the kennels — or
you'll both go."

"Thank you, sir," says the Master, grinning like a cat when she's safe behind the area railing.

"He's not a bad bull-terrier," says "Mr. Wyndham, sir," feeling my head. "Not that I know much about the smooth-coated breeds. My dogs are St. Bernards." He stopped patting me and held up my nose. "What's the matter with his ears?" he says. "They're chewed to pieces. Is this a fighting dog?" he asks, quick and rough-like.

I could have laughed. If he hadn't been holding my nose, I certainly would have had a good grin at him. Me the best under thirty pounds in the Province of Quebec, and him asking if I was a fighting dog! I ran to the Master and hung down my head modest-like, waiting for him to tell my list of battles; but the Master he coughs in his cap most painful. "Fightin' dawg, sir!" he cries. "Lor' bless you, sir, the Kid don't know the word. 'E's just a puppy, sir, same as you see; a pet dog, so to speak. 'E's a regular old lady's lap-dog, the Kid is."

"Well, you keep him away from my St. Bernards," says "Mr. Wyndham, sir," "or they might make a mouthful of him."

"Yes, sir; that they might," says the Master. But when we gets outside he slaps his knee and laughs inside hisself, and winks at me most sociable.

The Master's new home was in
the country, in a province they called
Long Island. There was a high stone
wall about his home with big iron
gates to it, same as Godfrey's brewery;
and there was a house with five red
roofs; and the stables, where I lived,
was cleaner than the aërated bakery-
shop. And then there was the kennels;
but they was like nothing else in this
world that ever I see. For the first
days I couldn't sleep of nights for fear
some one would catch me lying in
such a cleaned-up place, and would
chase me out of it; and when I did fall
to sleep I'd dream I was back in the
old Master's attic, shivering under the
rusty stove, which never had no coals

32

in it, with the Master flat on his back on the cold floor, with his clothes on. And I'd wake up scared and whimpering, and find myself on the new Master's cot with his hand on the quilt beside me; and I'd see the glow of the big stove, and hear the high-quality horses below-stairs stamping in their straw-lined boxes, and I'd snoop the sweet smell of hay and harness-soap and go to sleep again.

The stables was my jail, so the Master said, but I don't ask no better home than that jail.

"Now, Kid," says he, sitting on the top of a bucket upside down, "you've got to understand this. When I whistle it means you're not

33

to go out of this 'ere yard. These
stables is your jail. If you leave
'em I'll have to leave 'em too, and
over the seas, in the County Mayo,
an old mother will 'ave to leave her
bit of a cottage. For two pounds I
must be sending her every month, or
she'll have naught to eat, nor no
thatch over 'er head. I can't lose
my place, Kid, so see you don't lose
it for me. You must keep away
from the kennels," says he; " they're
not for the likes of you. The kennels
are for the quality. I wouldn't take
a litter of them woolly dogs for one
wag of your tail, Kid, but for all that
they are your betters, same as the
gentry up in the big house are my

34

betters. I know my place and keep away from the gentry, and you keep away from the champions."

So I never goes out of the stables. All day I just lay in the sun on the stone flags, licking my jaws, and watching the grooms wash down the carriages, and the only care I had was to see they didn't get gay and turn the hose on me. There wasn't even a single rat to plague me. Such stables I never did see.

"Nolan," says the head groom, "some day that dog of yours will give you the slip. You can't keep a street-dog tied up all his life. It's against his natur'." The head groom is a nice old gentleman, but he

35

doesn't know everything. Just as
though I'd been a street-dog because
I liked it! As if I'd rather poke for
my vittles in ash-heaps than have
'em handed me in a wash-basin, and
would sooner bite and fight than
be polite and sociable. If I'd had
mother there I couldn't have asked
for nothing more. But I'd think of
her snooping in the gutters, or freez-
ing of nights under the bridges, or,
what's worst of all, running through
the hot streets with her tongue down,
so wild and crazy for a drink that
the people would shout "mad dog"
at her and stone her. Water's so
good that I don't blame the men-
folks for locking it up inside their

36

houses ; but when the hot days come, I think they might remember that those are the dog-days, and leave a little water outside in a trough, like they do for the horses. Then we wouldn't go mad, and the policemen wouldn't shoot us. I had so much of everything I wanted that it made me think a lot of the days when I hadn't nothing, and if I could have given what I had to mother, as she used to share with me, I'd have been the happiest dog in the land. Not that I wasn't happy then, and most grateful to the Master, too, and if I'd only minded him, the trouble wouldn't have come again.

But one day the coachman says

that the little lady they called Miss
Dorothy had come back from school,
and that same morning she runs over
to the stables to pat her ponies, and
she sees me.

"Oh, what a nice little, white little
dog!" said she. "Whose little dog
are you?" says she.

"That's my dog, miss," says the
Master. "'Is name is Kid." And I
ran up to her most polite, and licks
her fingers, for I never see so pretty
and kind a lady.

"You must come with me and
call on my new puppies," says she,
picking me up in her arms and start-
ing off with me.

"Oh, but please, miss," cries

38

Nolan, "Mr. Wyndham give orders that the Kid's not to go to the kennels."

"That'll be all right," says the little lady; "they're my kennels too. And the puppies will like to play with him."

You wouldn't believe me if I was to tell you of the style of them quality-dogs. If I hadn't seen it myself I wouldn't have believed it neither. The Viceroy of Canada don't live no better. There was forty of them, but each one had his own house and a yard — most exclusive — and a cot and a drinking-basin all to hisself. They had servants standing round waiting to feed 'em when they was hungry, and valets to wash 'em; and they had their hair combed and brushed like the grooms must when they go out on the box. Even the puppies had overcoats with their names on 'em in blue letters, and the name of each of those they called champions was painted up fine over his front door just like it was a public house or a veterinary's. They were the biggest St. Bernards I ever did see. I could have walked under them if they'd have let me. But they were very proud and haughty dogs, and looked only once at me, and then sniffed in the air. The little lady's own dog was an old gentleman bull-dog. He'd come

40

along with us, and when he notices how taken aback I was with all I see, 'e turned quite kind and affable and showed me about.

"Jimmy Jocks," Miss Dorothy called him, but, owing to his weight, he walked most dignified and slow, waddling like a duck, as you might say, and looked much too proud and handsome for such a silly name.

"That's the runway, and that's the trophy-house," says he to me, "and that over there is the hospital, where you have to go if you get distemper, and the vet gives you beastly medicine."

"And which of these is your 'ouse, sir?" asks I, wishing to be respectful.

But he looked that hurt and haughty.
"I don't live in the kennels," says
he, most contemptuous. "I am a
house-dog. I sleep in Miss Dorothy's
room. And at lunch I'm let in with
the family, if the visitors don't mind.
They 'most always do, but they're
too polite to say so. Besides," says
he, smiling most condescending,
"visitors are always afraid of me.
It's because I'm so ugly," says he.
"I suppose," says he, screwing up
his wrinkles and speaking very slow
and impressive, "I suppose I'm the
ugliest bull-dog in America"; and as
he seemed to be so pleased to think
hisself so, I said, "Yes, sir; you
certainly are the ugliest ever I see,"

42

"I suppose I'm the ugliest bull-dog in America."

at which he nodded his head most
approving.

"But I couldn't hurt 'em, as you
say," he goes on, though I hadn't said
nothing like that, being too polite.
"I'm too old," he says; "I haven't
any teeth. The last time one of
those grizzly bears," said he, glaring
at the big St. Bernards, "took a hold
of me, he nearly was my death,"
says he. I thought his eyes would
pop out of his head, he seemed so
wrought up about it. "He rolled
me around in the dirt, he did," says
Jimmy Jocks, "an' I couldn't get up.
It was low," says Jimmy Jocks,
making a face like he had a bad
taste in his mouth. "Low, that's

what I call it — bad form, you understand, young man, not done in my set — and — and low." He growled 'way down in his stomach, and puffed hisself out, panting and blowing like he had been on a run.

"I'm not a street fighter," he says, scowling at a St. Bernard marked "Champion." "And when my rheumatism is not troubling me," he says, "I endeavor to be civil to all dogs, so long as they are gentlemen."

"Yes, sir," said I, for even to me he had been most affable.

At this we had come to a little house off by itself, and Jimmy Jocks invites me in. "This is their trophy-room," he says, "where they keep their

44

prizes. Mine," he says, rather grand-like, "are on the sideboard." Not knowing what a sideboard might be, I said, "Indeed, sir, that must be very gratifying." But he only wrinkled up his chops as much as to say, "It is my right."

The trophy-room was as wonderful as any public house I ever see. On the walls was pictures of nothing but beautiful St. Bernard dogs, and rows and rows of blue and red and yellow ribbons; and when I asked Jimmy Jocks why they was so many more of blue than of the others, he laughs and says, "Because these kennels always win." And there was many shining cups on the shelves,

which Jimmy Jocks told me were prizes won by the champions.

"Now, sir, might I ask you, sir," says I, "wot is a champion?"

At that he panted and breathed so hard I thought he would bust hisself. "My dear young friend!" says he, "wherever have you been educated? A champion is a — a champion," he says. "He must win nine blue ribbons in the 'open' class. You follow me — that is — against all comers. Then he has the title before his name, and they put his photograph in the sporting papers. You know, of course, that *I* am a champion," says he. "I am Champion Woodstock Wizard III, and the two other Woodstock

46

Wizards, my father and uncle, were both champions."

"But I thought your name was Jimmy Jocks," I said.

He laughs right out at that.

"That's my kennel name, not my registered name," he says. "Why, certainly you know that every dog has two names. Now, for instance, what's your registered name and number?" says he.

"I've got only one name," I says. "Just Kid."

Woodstock Wizard puffs at that and wrinkles up his forehead and pops out his eyes.

"Who are your people?" says he. "Where is your home?"

" At the stable, sir," I said. " My Master is the second groom."

At that Woodstock Wizard III looks at me for quite a bit without winking, and stares all around the room over my head.

" Oh, well," says he at last, " you're a very civil young dog," says he, " and I blame no one for what he can't help," which I thought most fair and liberal. " And I have known many bull-terriers that were champions," says he, " though as a rule they mostly run with fire-engines and to fighting. For me, I wouldn't care to run through the streets after a hose-cart, nor to fight," says he: " but each to his taste."

48

I could not help thinking that if Woodstock Wizard III tried to follow a fire-engine he would die of apoplexy, and seeing he'd lost his teeth, it was lucky he had no taste for fighting; but, after his being so condescending, I didn't say nothing.

"Anyway," says he, "every smooth-coated dog is better than any hairy old camel like those St. Bernards, and if ever you're hungry down at the stables, young man, come up to the house and I'll give you a bone. I can't eat them myself, but I bury them around the garden from force of habit and in case a friend should drop in. Ah, I see my mistress coming," he says, "and I bid

you good day. I regret," he says,
"that our different social position
prevents our meeting frequent, for
you're a worthy young dog with a
proper respect for your betters, and
in this country there's precious few
of them have that." Then he wad-
dles off, leaving me alone and very
sad, for he was the first dog in many
days that had spoke to me. But
since he showed, seeing that I was a
stable-dog, he didn't want my company, I waited for him to get well
away. It was not a cheerful place to
wait, the trophy-house. The pictures of the champions seemed to
scowl at me, and ask what right such
as I had even to admire them, and

50

the blue and gold ribbons and the silver cups made me very miserable. I had never won no blue ribbons or silver cups, only stakes for the old Master to spend in the publics; and I hadn't won them for being a beautiful high-quality dog, but just for fighting—which, of course, as Woodstock Wizard III says, is low. So I started for the stables, with my head down and my tail between my legs, feeling sorry I had ever left the Master. But I had more reason to be sorry before I got back to him.

The trophy-house was quite a bit from the kennels, and as I left it I see Miss Dorothy and Woodstock Wizard III walking back toward them, and, also, that a big St. Bernard, his name was Champion Red Elfberg, had broke his chain and was running their way. When he reaches old Jimmy Jocks he lets out a roar like a grain-steamer in a fog, and he makes three leaps for him. Old Jimmy Jocks was about a fourth his size; but he plants his feet and curves his back, and his hair goes up around his neck like a collar. But he never had no show at no time, for the grizzly bear, as Jimmy Jocks had called him, lights on old Jimmy's back and tries to break it, and old Jimmy Jocks snaps his gums and claws the grass, panting and groaning awful. But he can't do nothing,

52

and the grizzly bear just rolls him under him, biting and tearing cruel. The odds was all that Woodstock Wizard III was going to be killed; I had fought enough to see that: but not knowing the rules of the game among champions, I didn't like to interfere between two gentlemen who might be settling a private affair, and, as it were, take it as presuming of me. So I stood by, though I was shaking terrible, and holding myself in like I was on a leash. But at that Woodstock Wizard III, who was underneath, sees me through the dust, and calls very faint, "Help, you!" he says. "Take him in the hind leg," he says. "He's murdering me,"

he says. And then the little Miss
Dorothy, who was crying, and calling to the kennel-men, catches at the
Red Elfberg's hind legs to pull him
off, and the brute, keeping his front
pats well in Jimmy's stomach, turns
his big head and snaps at her. So
that was all I asked for, thank you.
I went up under him. It was really
nothing. He stood so high that I
had only to take off about three feet
from him and come in from the side,
and my long "punishing jaw," as
mother was always talking about,
locked on his woolly throat, and my
back teeth met. I couldn't shake
him, but I shook myself, and every
time I shook myself there was thirty

54

My long "punishing jaw" . . . locked on his woolly
throat.

pounds of weight tore at his wind-pipes. I couldn't see nothing for his long hair, but I heard Jimmy Jocks puffing and blowing on one side, and munching the brute's leg with his old gums. Jimmy was an old sport that day, was Jimmy, or Woodstock Wizard III, as I should say. When the Red Elfberg was out and down I had to run, or those kennel-men would have had my life. They chased me right into the stables; and from under the hay I watched the head groom take down a carriage-whip and order them to the right about. Luckily Master and the young grooms were out, or that day there'd have been fighting for everybody.

Well, it nearly did for me and the Master. "Mr. Wyndham, sir," comes raging to the stables. I'd half killed his best prize-winner, he says, and had oughter be shot, and he gives the Master his notice. But Miss Dorothy she follows him, and says it was his Red Elfberg what began the fight, and that I'd saved Jimmy's life, and that old Jimmy Jocks was worth more to her than all the St. Bernards in the Swiss mountains — wherever they may be. And that I was her champion, anyway. Then she cried over me most beautiful, and over Jimmy Jocks, too, who was that tied up in bandages he couldn't even waddle. So when he

56

heard that side of it, " Mr. Wyndham, sir," told us that if Nolan put
me on a chain we could stay. So it
came out all right for everybody but
me. I was glad the Master kept
his place, but I'd never worn a chain
before, and it disheartened me. But
that was the least of it. For the
quality-dogs couldn't forgive my
whipping their champion, and they
came to the fence between the kennels
and the stables, and laughed through
the bars, barking most cruel words
at me. I couldn't understand how
they found it out, but they knew.
After the fight Jimmy Jocks was most
condescending to me, and he said the
grooms had boasted to the kennel-

men that I was a son of Regent Royal, and that when the kennel-men asked who was my mother they had had to tell them that too. Perhaps that was the way of it, but, however, the scandal got out, and every one of the quality-dogs knew that I was a street-dog and the son of a black-and-tan.

"These misalliances will occur," said Jimmy Jocks, in his old-fashioned way; "but no well-bred dog," says he, looking most scornful at the St. Bernards, who were howling behind the palings, "would refer to your misfortune before you, certainly not cast it in your face. I myself remember your father's father, when

58

he made his début at the Crystal Palace. He took four blue ribbons and three specials."

But no sooner than Jimmy would leave me the St. Bernards would take to howling again, insulting mother and insulting me. And when I tore at my chain, they, seeing they were safe, would howl the more. It was never the same after that; the laughs and the jeers cut into my heart, and the chain bore heavy on my spirit. I was so sad that sometimes I wished I was back in the gutter again, where no one was better than me, and some nights I wished I was dead. If it hadn't been for the Master being so kind, and that it

would have looked like I was blaming mother, I would have twisted my leash and hanged myself.

About a month after my fight, the word was passed through the kennels that the New York Show was coming, and such goings on as followed I never did see. If each of them had been matched to fight for a thousand pounds and the gate, they couldn't have trained more conscientious. But perhaps that's just my envy. The kennel-men rubbed 'em and scrubbed 'em, and trims their hair and curls and combs it, and some dogs they fatted and some they starved. No one talked of nothing but the Show, and the chances

" our kennels " had against the other
kennels, and if this one of our champions would win over that one, and
whether them as hoped to be champions had better show in the " open "
or the " limit " class, and whether
this dog would beat his own dad, or
whether his little puppy sister couldn't
beat the two of 'em. Even the
grooms had their money up, and
day or night you heard nothing but
praises of " our " dogs, until I, being
so far out of it, couldn't have felt
meaner if I had been running the
streets with a can to my tail. I
knew shows were not for such as
me, and so all day I lay stretched at
the end of my chain, pretending I

was asleep, and only too glad that they had something so important to think of that they could leave me alone.

But one day, before the Show opened, Miss Dorothy came to the stables with "Mr. Wyndham, sir," and seeing me chained up and so miserable, she takes me in her arms.

"You poor little tyke!" says she. "It's cruel to tie him up so; he's eating his heart out, Nolan," she says. "I don't know nothing about bull-terriers," says she, "but I think Kid's got good points," says she, "and you ought to show him. Jimmy Jocks has three legs on the Rensselaer Cup now, and I'm going to show him this

62

time, so that he can get the fourth;
and, if you wish, I'll enter your dog
too. How would you like that,
Kid?" says she. "How would you
like to see the most beautiful dogs in
the world? Maybe you'd meet a
pal or two," says she. "It would
cheer you up, wouldn't it, Kid?" says
she. But I was so upset I could
only wag my tail most violent. "He
says it would!" says she, though,
being that excited, I hadn't said
nothing.

So "Mr. Wyndham, sir," laughs,
and takes out a piece of blue paper
and sits down at the head groom's
table.

"What's the name of the father of

your dog, Nolan?" says he. And Nolan says: "The man I got him off told me he was a son of Champion Regent Royal, sir. But it don't seem likely, does it?" says Nolan.

"It does not!" says "Mr. Wyndham, sir," short-like.

"Aren't you sure, Nolan?" says Miss Dorothy.

"No, miss," says the Master.

"Sire unknown," says "Mr. Wyndham, sir," and writes it down.

"Date of birth?" asks "Mr. Wyndham, sir."

"I—I—unknown, sir," says Nolan. And "Mr. Wyndham, sir," writes it down.

"Breeder?" says "Mr. Wyndham, sir."

64

"Unknown," says Nolan, getting very red around the jaws, and I drops my head and tail. And "Mr. Wyndham, sir," writes that down.

"Mother's name?" says "Mr. Wyndham, sir."

"She was a—unknown," says the Master. And I licks his hand.

"Dam unknown," says "Mr. Wyndham, sir," and writes it down. Then he takes the paper and reads out loud: "'Sire unknown, dam unknown, breeder unknown, date of birth unknown.' You'd better call him the 'Great Unknown,'" says he. "Who's paying his entrance fee?"

"I am," says Miss Dorothy.

Two weeks after we all got on a train for New York, Jimmy Jocks

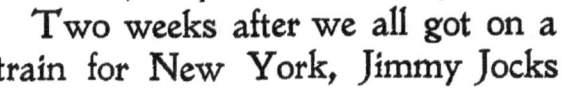

and me following Nolan in the smoking-car, and twenty-two of the St. Bernards in boxes and crates and on chains and leashes. Such a barking and howling I never did hear; and when they sees me going, too, they laughs fit to kill.

"Wot is this—a circus?" says the railroad man.

But I had no heart in it. I hated to go. I knew I was no "show" dog, even though Miss Dorothy and the Master did their best to keep me from shaming them. For before we set out Miss Dorothy brings a man from town who scrubbed and rubbed me, and sandpapered my tail, which hurt most awful, and

66

shaved my ears with the Master's razor, so you could 'most see clear through 'em, and sprinkles me over with pipe-clay, till I shines like a Tommy's cross-belts.

"Upon my word!" says Jimmy Jocks when he first sees me. "Wot a swell you are! You're the image of your grand-dad when he made his début at the Crystal Palace. He took four firsts and three specials." But I knew he was only trying to throw heart into me. They might scrub, and they might rub, and they might pipe-clay, but they couldn't pipe-clay the insides of me, and they was black-and-tan.

Then we came to a garden, which

67

it was not, but the biggest hall in the
world. Inside there was lines of
benches a few miles long, and on
them sat every dog in America. If
all the dog-snatchers in Montreal had
worked night and day for a year,
they couldn't have caught so many
dogs. And they was all shouting
and barking and howling so vicious
that my heart stopped beating. For
at first I thought they was all enraged
at my presuming to intrude. But after
I got in my place they kept at it just
the same, barking at every dog as he
come in: daring him to fight, and
ordering him out, and asking him
what breed of dog he thought he
was, anyway. Jimmy Jocks was

chained just behind me, and he said
he never see so fine a show. "That's
a hot class you're in, my lad," he
says, looking over into my street,
where there were thirty bull-terriers.
They was all as white as cream, and
each so beautiful that if I could have
broke my chain I would have run
all the way home and hid myself
under the horse-trough.

All night long they talked and sang,
and passed greetings with old pals,
and the homesick puppies howled
dismal. Them that couldn't sleep
wouldn't let no others sleep, and all
the electric lights burned in the roof,
and in my eyes. I could hear Jimmy
Jocks snoring peaceful, but I could

only doze by jerks, and when I dozed
I dreamed horrible. All the dogs in
the hall seemed coming at me for
daring to intrude, with their jaws red
and open, and their eyes blazing like
the lights in the roof. "You're a
street-dog! Get out, you street-dog!"
they yells. And as they drives me
out, the pipe-clay drops off me, and
they laugh and shriek; and when I
looks down I see that I have turned
into a black-and-tan.

They was most awful dreams, and
next morning, when Miss Dorothy
comes and gives me water in a pan,
I begs and begs her to take me home;
but she can't understand. "How
well Kid is!" she says. And when

70

"How well Kid is!" she says.

I jumps into the Master's arms and pulls to break my chain, he says, "If he knew all as he had against him, miss, he wouldn't be so gay." And from a book they reads out the names of the beautiful high-bred terriers which I have got to meet. And I can't make 'em understand that I only want to run away and hide myself where no one will see me.

Then suddenly men comes hurrying down our street and begins to brush the beautiful bull-terriers; and the Master rubs me with a towel so excited that his hands trembles awful, and Miss Dorothy tweaks my ears between her gloves, so that the blood runs to 'em, and they turn pink and stand up straight and sharp.

"Now, then, Nolan," says she, her voice shaking just like his fingers, "keep his head up—and never let the judge lose sight of him." When I hears that my legs breaks under me, for I knows all about judges. Twice the old Master goes up before the judge for fighting me with other dogs, and the judge promises him if he ever does it again he'll chain him up in jail. I knew he'd find me out. A judge can't be fooled by no pipe-clay. He can see right through you, and he reads your insides.

The judging-ring, which is where the judge holds out, was so like a

72

fighting-pit that when I come in it, and find six other dogs there, I springs into position, so that when they lets us go I can defend myself. But the Master smooths down my hair and whispers, " Hold 'ard, Kid, hold 'ard. This ain't a fight," says he. "Look your prettiest," he whispers. "Please, Kid, look your prettiest "; and he pulls my leash so tight that I can't touch my pats to the sawdust, and my nose goes up in the air. There was millions of people a-watching us from the railings, and three of our kennel-men, too, making fun of the Master and me, and Miss Dorothy with her chin just reaching to the rail, and her eyes so big that I thought she

73

was a-going to cry. It was awful to think that when the judge stood up and exposed me, all those people, and Miss Dorothy, would be there to see me driven from the Show.

The judge he was a fierce-looking man with specs on his nose, and a red beard. When I first come in he didn't see me, owing to my being too quick for him and dodging behind the Master. But when the Master drags me round and I pulls at the sawdust to keep back, the judge looks at us careless-like, and then stops and glares through his specs, and I knew it was all up with me.

"Are there any more?" asks the

74

judge to the gentleman at the gate, but never taking his specs from me.

The man at the gate looks in his book. "Seven in the novice class," says he. "They're all here. You can go ahead," and he shuts the gate.

The judge he doesn't hesitate a moment. He just waves his hand toward the corner of the ring. "Take him away," he says to the Master, "over there, and keep him away"; and he turns and looks most solemn at the six beautiful bull-terriers. I don't know how I crawled to that corner. I wanted to scratch under the sawdust and dig myself a grave. The kennel-men they slapped the rail with their hands and laughed

75

at the Master like they would fall over. They pointed at me in the corner, and their sides just shaked. But little Miss Dorothy she presses her lips tight against the rail, and I see tears rolling from her eyes. The Master he hangs his head like he had been whipped. I felt most sorry for him than all. He was so red, and he was letting on not to see the kennel-men, and blinking his eyes. If the judge had ordered me right out it wouldn't have disgraced us so, but it was keeping me there while he was judging the high-bred dogs that hurt so hard. With all those people staring, too. And his doing it so quick, without no doubt nor questions. You

76

can't fool the judges. They see inside
you.

But he couldn't make up his mind
about them high-bred dogs. He
scowls at 'em, and he glares at 'em,
first with his head on the one side and
then on the other. And he feels of 'em,
and orders 'em to run about. And
Nolan leans against the rails, with his
head hung down, and pats me. And
Miss Dorothy comes over beside him,
but don't say nothing, only wipes her
eye with her finger. A man on the
other side of the rail he says to the Master, "The judge don't like your dog?"

"No," says the Master.

"Have you ever shown him before?" says the man.

"No," says the Master, "and I'll never show him again. He's my dog," says the Master, "and he suits me! And I don't care what no judges think." And when he says them kind words, I licks his hand most grateful.

The judge had two of the six dogs on a little platform in the middle of the ring, and he had chased the four other dogs into the corners, where they was licking their chops, and letting on they didn't care, same as Nolan was.

The two dogs on the platform was so beautiful that the judge hisself couldn't tell which was the best of 'em, even when he stoops down

78

and holds their heads together. But at last he gives a sigh, and brushes the sawdust off his knees, and goes to the table in the ring, where there was a man keeping score, and heaps and heaps of blue and gold and red and yellow ribbons. And the judge picks up a bunch of 'em and walks to the two gentlemen who was holding the beautiful dogs, and he says to each, "What's his number?" and he hands each gentleman a ribbon. And then he turned sharp and comes straight at the Master.

"What's his number?" says the judge. And Master was so scared that he couldn't make no answer.

But Miss Dorothy claps her hands

and cries out like she was laughing,
"Three twenty-six," and the judge
writes it down and shoves Master
the blue ribbon.

I bit the Master, and I jumps and
bit Miss Dorothy, and I waggled so
hard that the Master couldn't hold
me. When I get to the gate Miss
Dorothy snatches me up and kisses
me between the ears, right before
millions of people, and they both hold
me so tight that I didn't know which
of them was carrying of me. But
one thing I knew, for I listened hard,
as it was the judge hisself as said it.

"Did you see that puppy I gave
first to?" says the judge to the
gentleman at the gate.

80

"I did. He was a bit out of his class," says the gate gentleman.

"He certainly was!" says the judge, and they both laughed.

But I didn't care. They couldn't hurt me then, not with Nolan holding the blue ribbon and Miss Dorothy hugging my ears, and the kennel-men sneaking away, each looking like he'd been caught with his nose under the lid of the slop-can.

We sat down together, and we all three just talked as fast as we could. They was so pleased that I couldn't help feeling proud myself, and I barked and leaped about so gay that all the bull-terriers in our street stretched on their chains and howled at me.

" Just look at him!" says one of
those I had beat. " What's he giving
hisself airs about?"

" Because he's got one blue ribbon!" says another of 'em. " Why,
when I was a puppy I used to eat
'em, and if that judge could ever
learn to know a toy from a mastiff,
I'd have had this one."

But Jimmy Jocks he leaned over
from his bench and says, " Well done,
Kid. Didn't I tell you so?" What
he 'ad told me was that I might get a
" commended," but I didn't remind
him.

" Didn't I tell you," says Jimmy
Jocks, " that I saw your grandfather
make his début at the Crystal —"

"Yes, sir, you did, sir," says I, for I have no love for the men of my family.

A gentleman with a showing-leash around his neck comes up just then and looks at me very critical. "Nice dog you've got, Miss Wyndham," says he; "would you care to sell him?"

"He's not my dog," says Miss Dorothy, holding me tight. "I wish he were."

"He's not for sale, sir," says the Master, and I was *that* glad.

"Oh, he's yours, is he?" says the gentleman, looking hard at Nolan. "Well, I'll give you a hundred dollars for him," says he, careless-like.

"Thank you, sir; he's not for sale,"
says Nolan, but his eyes get very big.
The gentleman he walked away; but
I watches him, and he talks to a man
in a golf-cap, and by and by the man
comes along our street, looking at all
the dogs, and stops in front of me.

"This your dog?" says he to
Nolan. "Pity he's so leggy," says
he. "If he had a good tail, and a
longer stop, and his ears were set
higher, he'd be a good dog. As he
is, I'll give you fifty dollars for him."

But, before the Master could speak,
Miss Dorothy laughs and says:
"You're Mr. Polk's kennel-man, I
believe. Well, you tell Mr. Polk
from me that the dog's not for sale

84

now any more than he was five min-
utes ago, and that when he is, he'll
have to bid against me for him."

The man looks foolish at that, but
he turns to Nolan quick-like. "I'll
give you three hundred for him," he
says.

"Oh, indeed!" whispers Miss
Dorothy, like she was talking to herself. "That's it, is it?" And she turns
and looks at me just as though she
had never seen me before. Nolan
he was a-gaping, too, with his mouth
open. But he holds me tight.

"He's not for sale," he growls,
like he was frightened; and the man
looks black and walks away.

"Why, Nolan!" cries Miss Dorothy, "Mr. Polk knows more about bull-terriers than any amateur in America. What can he mean? Why, Kid is no more than a puppy! Three hundred dollars for a puppy!"

"And he ain't no thoroughbred, neither!" cries the Master. "He's 'Unknown,' ain't he? Kid can't help it, of course, but his mother, miss—"

I dropped my head. I couldn't bear he should tell Miss Dorothy. I couldn't bear she should know I had stolen my blue ribbon.

But the Master never told, for at that a gentleman runs up, calling, "Three twenty-six, three twenty-six!" And Miss Dorothy says, "Here he is; what is it?"

86

"The Winners' class," says the gentleman. "Hurry, please; the judge is waiting for him."

Nolan tries to get me off the chain on to a showing-leash, but he shakes so, he only chokes me. "What is it, miss?" he says. "What is it?"

"The Winners' class," says Miss Dorothy. "The judge wants him with the winners of the other classes — to decide which is the best. It's only a form," says she. "He has the champions against him now."

"Yes," says the gentleman, as he hurries us to the ring. "I'm afraid it's only a form for your dog, but the judge wants all the winners, puppy class even."

We had got to the gate, and the

87

gentleman there was writing down
my number.

"Who won the open?" asks
Miss Dorothy.

"Oh, who would?" laughs the
gentleman. "The old champion, of
course. He's won for three years
now. There he is. Isn't he wonderful?" says he; and he points to
a dog that's standing proud and
haughty on the platform in the
middle of the ring.

I never see so beautiful a dog — so
fine and clean and noble, so white
like he had rolled hisself in flour,
holding his nose up and his eyes shut,
same as though no one was worth
looking at. Aside of him we other

88

dogs, even though we had a blue ribbon apiece, seemed like lumps of mud. He was a royal gentleman, a king, he was. His master didn't have to hold his head with no leash. He held it hisself, standing as still as an iron dog on a lawn, like he knew all the people was looking at him. And so they was, and no one around the ring pointed at no other dog but him.

"Oh, what a picture!" cried Miss Dorothy. "He's like a marble figure by a great artist — one who loved dogs. Who is he?" says she, looking in her book. "I don't keep up with terriers."

"Oh, you know him," says the

gentleman. "He is the champion of champions, Regent Royal."

The Master's face went red.

"And this is Regent Royal's son," cries he, and he pulls me quick into the ring, and plants me on the platform next my father.

I trembled so that I near fell. My legs twisted like a leash. But my father he never looked at me. He only smiled the same sleepy smile, and he still kept his eyes half shut, like as no one, no, not even his own son, was worth his lookin' at.

The judge he didn't let me stay beside my father, but, one by one, he placed the other dogs next to him and measured and felt and pulled at them.

90

And each one he put down, but he never put my father down. And then he comes over and picks up me and sets me back on the platform, shoulder to shoulder with the Champion Regent Royal, and goes down on his knees, and looks into our eyes.

The gentleman with my father he laughs, and says to the judge, "Thinking of keeping us here all day, John?" But the judge he doesn't hear him, and goes behind us and runs his hand down my side, and holds back my ears, and takes my jaws between his fingers. The crowd around the ring is very deep now, and nobody says nothing. The gentleman at the score-table, he is leaning forward, with his elbows on his knees and his eyes very wide, and the gentleman at the gate is whispering quick to Miss Dorothy, who has turned white. I stood as stiff as stone. I didn't even breathe. But out of the corner of my eye I could see my father licking his pink chops, and yawning just a little, like he was bored.

The judge he had stopped looking fierce and was looking solemn. Something inside him seemed a-troubling him awful. The more he stares at us now, the more solemn he gets, and when he touches us he does it gentle, like he was patting us. For a long time he kneels in the sawdust, looking at my father and at me, and

92

For a long time he kneels in the sawdust.

no one around the ring says nothing to nobody.

Then the judge takes a breath and touches me sudden. "It's his," he says. But he lays his hand just as quick on my father. "I'm sorry," says he.

The gentleman holding my father cries :

"Do you mean to tell me —"

And the judge he answers, "I mean the other is the better dog." He takes my father's head between his hands and looks down at him most sorrowful. "The king is dead," says he. "Long live the king! Good-by, Regent," he says.

The crowd around the railings

clapped their hands, and some laughed scornful, and every one talks fast, and I start for the gate, so dizzy that I can't see my way. But my father pushes in front of me, walking very daintily, and smiling sleepy, same as he had just been waked, with his head high and his eyes shut, looking at nobody.

So that is how I " came by my inheritance," as Miss Dorothy calls it; and just for that, though I couldn't feel where I was any different, the crowd follows me to my bench, and pats me, and coos at me, like I was a baby in a baby-carriage. And the handlers have to hold 'em back so that the gentlemen from the papers

94

can make pictures of me, and Nolan walks me up and down so proud, and the men shake their heads and says, "He certainly is the true type, he is!" And the pretty ladies ask Miss Dorothy, who sits beside me letting me lick her gloves to show the crowd what friends we is, "Aren't you afraid he'll bite you?" And Jimmy Jocks calls to me, "Didn't I tell you so? I always knew you were one of us. Blood will out, Kid; blood will out. I saw your grandfather," says he, "make his début at the Crystal Palace. But he was never the dog you are!"

After that, if I could have asked for it, there was nothing I couldn't get.

You might have thought I was a snow-dog, and they was afeard I'd melt. If I wet my pats, Nolan gave me a hot bath and chained me to the stove; if I couldn't eat my food, being stuffed full by the cook,—for I am a house-dog now, and let in to lunch, whether there is visitors or not,— Nolan would run to bring the vet. It was all tommy rot, as Jimmy says, but meant most kind. I couldn't scratch myself comfortable, without Nolan giving me nasty drinks, and rubbing me outside till it burnt awful; and I wasn't let to eat bones for fear of spoiling my "beautiful" mouth, what mother used to call my " punishing jaw"; and my food was cooked special

96

on a gas-stove; and Miss Dorothy
gives me an overcoat, cut very stylish like the champions', to wear when
we goes out carriage-driving.

After the next Show, where I takes
three blue ribbons, four silver cups,
two medals, and brings home forty-
five dollars for Nolan, they gives me
a "registered" name, same as Jimmy's. Miss Dorothy wanted to call
me "Regent Heir Apparent"; but I
was *that* glad when Nolan says,
"No; Kid don't owe nothing to his
father, only to you and hisself. So,
if you please, miss, we'll call him
Wyndham Kid." And so they did,
and you can see it on my overcoat in
blue letters, and painted top of my

97

kennel. It was all too hard to understand. For days I just sat and won-
dered if I was really me, and how it
all come about, and why everybody
was so kind. But oh, it was so good
they was, for if they hadn't been I'd
never have got the thing I most
wished after. But, because they was
kind, and not liking to deny me nothing, they gave it me, and it was more
to me than anything in the world.

It came about one day when we
was out driving. We was in the
cart they calls the dog-cart because
it's the one Miss Dorothy keeps to
take Jimmy and me for an airing.
Nolan was up behind, and me, in my
new overcoat, was sitting beside Miss

98

Dorothy. I was admiring the view, and thinking how good it was to have a horse pull you about so that you needn't get yourself splashed and have to be washed, when I hears a dog calling loud for help, and I pricks up my ears and looks over the horse's head. And I sees something that makes me tremble down to my toes. In the road before us three big dogs was chasing a little old lady-dog. She had a string to her tail, where some boys had tied a can, and she was dirty with mud and ashes, and torn most awful. She was too far done up to get away, and too old to help herself, but she was making a fight for her life, snapping her old gums

99

savage, and dying game. All this I
see in a wink, and then the three dogs
pinned her down, and I can't stand it
no longer, and clears the wheel and
lands in the road on my head. It
was my stylish overcoat done that,
and I cursed it proper, but I gets my
pats again quick, and makes a rush
for the fighting. Behind me I hear
Miss Dorothy cry: " They'll kill that
old dog. Wait, take my whip. Beat
them off her! The Kid can take care
of himself"; and I hear Nolan fall into
the road, and the horse come to a
stop. The old lady-dog was down, and
the three was eating her vicious; but
as I come up, scattering the pebbles,
she hears, and thinking it's one more

of them, she lifts her head, and my
heart breaks open like some one had
sunk his teeth in it. For, under the
ashes and the dirt and the blood, I
can see who it is, and I know that
my mother has come back to me.

I gives a yell that throws them
three dogs off their legs.

"Mother!" I cries. "I'm the
Kid," I cries. "I'm coming to you.
Mother, I'm coming!"

And I shoots over her at the throat
of the big dog, and the other two
they sinks their teeth into that stylish
overcoat and tears it off me, and that
sets me free, and I lets them have it.
I never had so fine a fight as that!
What with mother being there to see,

and not having been let to mix up in no fights since I become a prize-winner, it just naturally did me good, and it wasn't three shakes before I had 'em yelping. Quick as a wink, mother she jumps in to help me, and I just laughed to see her. It was so like old times. And Nolan he made me laugh, too. He was like a hen on a bank, shaking the butt of his whip, but not daring to cut in for fear of hitting me.

"Stop it, Kid," he says, "stop it. Do you want to be all torn up?" says he. "Think of the Boston show," says he. "Think of Chicago. Think of Danbury. Don't you never want to be a champion?"

How was I to think of all them places when I had three dogs to cut up at the same time? But in a minute two of 'em begs for mercy, and mother and me lets 'em run away. The big one he ain't able to run away. Then mother and me we dances and jumps, and barks and laughs, and bites each other and rolls each other in the road. There never was two dogs so happy as we. And Nolan he whistles and calls and begs me to come to him; but I just laugh and play larks with mother.

"Now, you come with me," says I, "to my new home, and never try to run away again." And I shows her our house with the five red roofs, set on the top of the hill. But mother trembles awful, and says: "They'd never let me in such a place. Does the Viceroy live there, Kid?" says she. And I laugh at her. "No; I do," I says. "And if they won't let you live there, too, you and me will go back to the streets together, for we must never be parted no more." So we trots up the hill side by side, with Nolan trying to catch me, and Miss Dorothy laughing at him from the cart.

"The Kid's made friends with the poor old dog," says she. "Maybe he knew her long ago when he ran the streets himself. Put her in here beside me, and see if he doesn't follow."

104

So when I hears that I tells mother
to go with Nolan and sit in the cart;
but she says no — that she'd soil the
pretty lady's frock; but I tells her to
do as I say, and so Nolan lifts her,
trembling still, into the cart, and I
runs alongside, barking joyful.

When we drives into the stables I
takes mother to my kennel, and tells
her to go inside it and make herself
at home. "Oh, but he won't let
me!" says she.

"Who won't let you?" says I,
keeping my eye on Nolan, and growl-
ing a bit nasty, just to show I was
meaning to have my way.

"Why, Wyndham Kid," says she,
looking up at the name on my kennel.

"But I'm Wyndham Kid!" says I.

"You!" cries mother. "You! Is my little Kid the great Wyndham Kid the dogs all talk about?" And at that, she being very old, and sick, and nervous, as mothers are, just drops down in the straw and weeps bitter.

Well, there ain't much more than that to tell. Miss Dorothy she settled it.

"If the Kid wants the poor old thing in the stables," says she, "let her stay.

"You see," says she, "she's a black-and-tan, and his mother was a black-and-tan, and maybe that's what makes Kid feel so friendly toward her," says she.

106

"Indeed, for me," says Nolan, "she can have the best there is. I'd never drive out no dog that asks for a crust nor a shelter," he says. "But what will Mr. Wyndham do?"

"He'll do what I say," says Miss Dorothy, "and if I say she's to stay, she will stay, and I say — she's to stay!"

And so mother and Nolan and me found a home. Mother was scared at first — not being used to kind people; but she was so gentle and loving that the grooms got fonder of her than of me, and tried to make me jealous by patting of her and giving her the pick of the vittles. But that was the wrong way to hurt

107